Some wisdom an eastern culture

The Black Swan

Happy Easter
Love
Mom

Anthony Aikman

POST
BOOKS

The Black Swan

Published by Post Books, The Post Publishing Plc.

136 Na Ranong Road, off Sunthorn Kosa Road,

Klong Toey, Bangkok 10110, Thailand

Tel. (662) 240-3700 ext. 1691-2

Fax. (662) 671-9698

e-mail: postbooks@bangkokpost.co.th

http: //www.bangkokpost.net/postbooks/

Text and illustrations © Anthony Aikman 1999

First published in Thailand in 1999

Printed by Allied Printers, The Post Publishing Plc.

National Library of Thailand Cataloging-in-Publication Data

Aikman, Anthony.

The Black Swan. — Bangkok : Post Books, 1999. 152 p.

1. Tales. I. Title. 398.2

ISBN: 974-202-049-3

Design: Darunee Lertwatthana

Set in: CoventryScript, Helvetica Light, RegencyScript and Times

With grateful thanks to Reverend Stephen Easter
whose encouragement and example has
strengthened the hopes and faith of many people.

Contents

The Garden

A very long time ago — so long it might just have been yesterday, God planted a Garden. It lay within a curve of a great sandy river. Fruit bats hung upside down from the top-most branches cooling themselves in the breeze in the heat of the day, while at evening elephants rolled in the shallows squirting water over themselves. In the Garden God gathered together plants and animals from all over the face of the Earth.

God planted a garden

A Black Swan carried them there. Like a messenger he brought them by seed and seedling, by eggs and buds and newborn, carrying them safely in his beak and between the strong webs of his feet. He placed them where each would thrive best. He brought the double-fruited coconut that men call 'Coco du Mer' from the desert isles of coral seas, fat bellied baobabs from Africa, giant bamboo from eastern forests which he planted along the river bank — their towering shoots soaring skywards over the stream.

He planted fig trees whose roots snaked through the long grass scented and speckled with pungent herbs and wild exotic flowers. He planted forest trees whose fluted trunks fanned like wings, tall trees crested with palms or branches spanned like the spars of square-rigged ships.

Orchids sprayed clusters of colour from amid the fronds of sombre ferns.

plants and animals from everywhere

Over everything hung the sky full of blue vigour with ever-changing clouds towering up and sailing through. Eagles swayed on air currents, high above the jungled hills, cataracts plunged into green depths, howler monkeys swung in the branches, butterflies fluttered above bright leaves, darting humming birds sipped the scented flowers, cicadas shrilled in the stillness, panthers prowled in the shadows.

The Black Swan carried a small child to the Garden and placed him safely afloat in the circular boat leaf of the giant Amazonian water lily.

"Are you my father?" the boy asked one day when the Swan came to see him.

"No," replied the Swan. "But I will protect you."

a Black Swan carried them

"You are the father of all things," suggested the boy another day as he lay among the black down of the Swan's broad back.

"No," replied the Swan, "I am just a messenger but I fly on the winds of God."

"Who is God?" asked the boy.

"God is the source of all things; God is before anything ever *was*."

"God is the Word that is the source of all words, the knower who is the source of all knowledge. No one can ever know Him but He is in us and we are in Him. We come from Him and to Him we return."

But the boy did not hear him. He had fallen softly asleep in the warmth of the sun. The boy grew into a sturdy lad living in harmony with all the plants and animals of the garden who knew him as a friend, not as a threat.

living in harmony

"I can climb a tree just like you," he shouted up to the howler monkey. "But not so fast," chattered back the monkey.

"I can jump and swing from the branches just like you," he call out to the orangutan. "But not so far," smiled back the hairy red ape.

"But I can't fly like you," he said wistfully, watching the birds soaring in the sky. "Or like you," to the dragonfly hovering over the floating lilies.

"I wish I could fly," said the boy. He was sitting astride a bough overhanging the river. "Perhaps if I stand on tip-toe and stretch upwards ..." The boy stepped on the branch, balancing until just the tips of his toes touched. He closed his eyes tight-shut and for an instant he imagined himself floating. Then with a loud splash he fell into the river.

I wish I could fly

The Black Swan, flying low, scooped up the boy between its swarthy webs and dropped him gently on the river bank.

"Why can't I fly?" the boy asked the Swan. "Leaves don't have wings and they fly."

"If you want to feel light as air," suggested the Swan gently, "what sort of thoughts fill your head?"

"Nice thoughts," said the boy softly and closing his eyes he filled his head with bright glimmers of joy and peace so that his mind seemed to float like airy bubbles.

"If only I could fill all of me like that," sighed the boy doubtfully. "But these other thoughts come along — heavy, unkind thoughts that seem to grab my ankles and pull me down." The boy leaned against the strong folded wing of the Black Swan and glumly watched a leaf floating downstream.

the sky is so vast

He slipped naked into the shallows and taking a deep breath stretched his body out on the water. Sunlight dappled his brown body. He floated effortlessly, gazing up through the foliage to the blue sky high above.

"Why is the sky so vast?" he asked the Black Swan swimming beside him.

"The sky is a word of God," replied the Swan. "Like the sea and the wind and the mountain."

"A very big word," said the boy thoughtfully.

"Just as you are a very small word."

"And the leaf is an even smaller word," laughed the boy. Then, puzzled, he asked, "But what of the words we speak? Are they all fragments of a big word?"

"Better than a thousand useless words," answered the Swan quietly, "is one single word that gives peace."

in God is no darkness at all

"And do all the words of God float?" enquired the boy, squinting skywards, his limbs splayed out motionless on the shining surface of the water.

"Like light shining in darkness," said the Swan. "God *is* Light" he continued. "In Him is no darkness at all. If you swim towards light you find life — but if you choose to plunge into darkness ...."

"Oooah," said the boy, scared, doubling up and instantly sinking. He surfaced spluttering and sat clutching his knees in the shallows. "But what is the dark? The night is dark."

"No, the night is not dark," said the Swan. "Not with the stars and moon to brighten it. Darkness is the hatred and evil that can fill people's hearts so that they can no longer live in harmony."

"I cannot imagine that" said the boy, "because I have never seen it."

"You have never been out of the Garden," said the Swan. "Perhaps I should show you; then you will know how lucky you are."

the night is not dark

"Perhaps," agreed the boy doubtfully, "but only if you promise to bring me back."

"When you are ready," promised the Swan, "I will bring you back. Now climb up between my wings and carefully put your arms around my neck." Then, beating his powerful wings, the Swan rose up into the sky, until the river and trees lay far, far below.

"Where are we going?" cried the boy, dazzled and breathless but delighted to be airborne nonetheless.

"We are going to the City," called back the Swan.

"I have never seen a City" the boy shouted in exhilaration, his hair blown back by the wind.

"You may not like it," murmured the Swan, lifting his wings in a graceful arch and soaring away towards the west.

where are we going?

Below them the forest vanished, replaced by a patchwork of fields that in turn gave way to lines of streets and row upon row of houses.

They circled slowly above the City while the sun settled lower in the sky. The boy became alarmed. "But why must I go to the City?" he pleaded sadly, his head pressed to the Swan's neck.

Without turning the Swan answered, "You cannot stay forever in the Garden without living in the City for a while. And when you are there," added the Swan, "...remember that what you do is not always as important as the way you do it."

"But if I do it all wrong?" cried the boy, "You'll be angry and perhaps you won't let me come back."

off to town

"Nobody ever does it *all* wrong," comforted the Swan. "And I will not be angry, for I understand the temptations of the City and the weakness of people's hearts."

"But how will I know?" said the boy, despairing as he stared down at the unfamiliar city milling with strange people.

"You will know," insisted the Black Swan, "For although you may not see me, I will be there at your side. You will not be alone if you remember that. You will only feel alone if you do something you know I would not like — that you cannot share with me. Then you will feel as if you want to hide from me."

"Oh, no, never!" cried the boy in alarm.

"Although we don't realise it at the time," continued the Swan, circling lower over the City, "whenever we give in to greed or anger or desire we lose something, we become a little less, just as a tree loses its leaves when the storm blows. Only God can restore us, give us back what we have lost, make us whole again."

only God can restore us

"And will He?" asked the boy, worried.

"Oh yes," assured the Swan, "Out of love He will always redeem us so long as we confide in Him and open our heart to Him."

The boy thought for a while, "But doesn't God get irritated if we constantly pester Him?"

The Swan smiled at him. "Like when you are hot and the flies come and settle on you seeking a little of your sustenance and you brush them off? No, God will not brush you off, no matter how many come crowding to Him seeking His sustenance — for that is the food of Eternal Life."

The Swan began to descend. "Remember this too," he said. "Even when you shield your eyes from the glare of the sun and search for the speck of my shadow against the sky and still cannot find me — I have not left you. I shall always be watching over you. But I will not interfere with anything you choose to do."

I have not left you ...

The Black Swan glided down towards a muddy river bordering the City and landed softly in the shadows. A few strokes of his powerful webbed feet brought them to the bank.

The boy got off and stood uncertainly among the tall reeds. The Swan smiled back at him.

"Do not be afraid. I promise you that, no matter how far you stray, you can always return. I will always welcome you back as if you were my own child."

As the boy stumbled up the muddy bank, trying to hold back his tears, the Swan called out a final time. "Try to choose for friends those whose soul is beautiful, try to go only with those whose soul is good."

And then as he unfolded his great wings and prepared to fly away he added, "And look upon the person who tells you your faults as if he told you of a hidden treasure."

he turned to face the City

With powerful strokes the Black Swan soared aloft and vanished into the dusk.

The boy turned and faced the City.

After the familiar quiet of the Garden the unexpected chaos and havoc and splendour of the City burst around him like a thousand firecrackers.

The City

The first thing to alarm him was the busy traffic; cars and motorbikes seemed to roar by in all directions and when he tried to cross the street everything seemed intent on running him down.

As he dodged the puddles and potholes of a side street, people were too busy with their own concerns to notice him. The pedalling cyclo drivers trying to get a fare, the barefoot children collecting refuse — searching for anything they could sell; girls tugging water carts bigger than themselves;

but no one noticed

balloon sellers, pedlars, knife sharpeners, women with large wicker baskets, full of bread. No one seemed to have time to spare to answer any of his questions.

"But where am I?" he cried.

"Where do you think?" bawled back an evening jogger dashing past and disappearing into the crowd. "But what is everyone doing?" persisted the boy.

"Making money, what else?" answered a man squatting down mending tyres.

"Money?" queried the boy. "Will money help me to fly?" for he had the sudden wish to escape from the City as quickly as he could.

The driver of the waiting car wound down the window of his white limousine. "With money," he grinned, flashing gold teeth, gold bracelet, gold wristwatch, "with money you won't want to fly. You'll be happy to stay around and make more."

money – can I eat it?

"What's money? Can I eat it?" asked the boy, who was feeling quite hungry.

The driver and the repair man both guffawed.

"No," said the repair man as he bolted back on the wheel. "But without it you can't eat."

"Food don't grow out of the ground in a City, boy," growled the driver. "This ain't the country. Here you have to *buy* food. Buying means money."

"How do I get money?" asked the boy curiously.

"What have you got to sell?" said the driver.

"Nothing — I've just got here. I'm on my own."

The driver looked at him sternly. "Don't say that aloud in a city, boy, — people might take advantage. Anyway," he added, "You can always beg. If you can't buy or borrow, then you beg," he quipped as he paid the repair man and drove off.

room with a view ...

Further down the road where a market was closing for the night, street children were helping themselves to fruit and leftovers that had been thrown onto a big smelly heap.

The boy joined in uninvited. Later they all settled down to sleep near the shelter of a pagoda. The boy got quite bitten with bugs and fleas but before dawn everyone was up and ready with their sacks for a day's collecting.

"Cans and plastic bottles are best," they told him. "But you won't know where to sell it — so you'd better follow us."

It was hot and tiring walking along the dirty, dusty streets, poking about in the refuse heaps. The boy had no shoes and his feet ached. The sun burned down overhead.

off to work

How he longed for the cool shade of the Garden. Here too there was a river — a broad, muddy, dirty river where they all gathered at midday to wash and swim. Cyclo drivers were scrubbing their clothes before putting them back on, ragged begging women were washing their infants and the garbage kids were happily splashing. Regrettably the bank was also the local toilet but this didn't stop their delight at leaping into the water.

In the evening they all hauled their heavy sacks to a yard piled high with refuse sorted into untidy heaps of cardboard, wire, plastic, and cans. A yard man sneered derisively at the contents of the boy's sack. Coins jingled in his hand and he tossed one to the boy. The boy felt bitterly disappointed.

"I worked all day just for this," he complained.

to have or have not

A trader loading his pick-up truck regarded him. "Son," he said, "It's called the Law of Unequal Opportunities."

He paused to light a cigarette.

"There's the *have's* which is me and the *have-nots*, nor ever likely to have — which is you. Let me educate you. Maybe what you want for yourself is as important as what I want for myself. Priorities are equal — except that the more important you get the more important seem to be your priorities.

"But the difference lies with expectations — I'm going to achieve mine and you're not. Oh, I know you work a lot harder collecting cans than I do selling them — but I'm going to make money and you are not." He chuckled. "Not unless you win the lottery — but I don't expect you can afford a ticket."

supper for some

With this cryptic lesson in human economics ringing in his ears the boy picked his way wearily back to the market. Women sat ladling boiled rice from big cauldrons. The coin the boy earned would barely buy him a decent plateful.

The next morning before they set off he noticed a line of men and boys in yellow robes stepping barefoot along the street.

They carried large covered bowls which housewives and shopkeepers hurried out to fill with rice and food, bowing low as they did so. Others knelt down and placed money in the men's bags.

"Who are they?" asked the boy. "Can I do that?"

The others laughed. "They are monks. You are not a monk or a novice."

"But what is a monk?" asked the boy, curious.

breakfast for others

"A monk is a holy man — he prays to God, he lives a good life."

"And I cannot pray to God?" queried the boy.

"I suppose anyone can pray," his companion replied. "But monks know how to best. They pray to God in this ancient tongue. They know more about God — and they have time to pray all the time."

"And they don't collect garbage and people give them food," quipped the boy. "So how does one become a monk?"

None of the kids knew but they thought one would go and live at the local temple.

"It's not so easy," they told him. "You can't eat after mid-day and you can't play games and you have to get up to pray at 4 o'clock in the morning."

But before the boy could decide to be a monk he was just as curious of the long lines of neatly dressed children who morning and afternoon streamed through the streets on foot or by bicycle, dressed in pressed white shirts, and blue skirts or trousers.

sacks or satchels

The garbage collectors thought he was utterly stupid. "They go to school."

And in reply to his questions added, "No, of course no one pays them. They learn things. They learn to read and write and add things up. They are not like us."

"But all of us would go to school if we could."

"If you go to school," explained one, "You'll get a good job later, own a car, a nice house. You won't live in a shack." He sighed. "Perhaps in the next life I'll be born in a rich house and go to school."

All day long as he toiled, dragging his heavy sack along the dirty streets the boy thought about this.

the other life

Sometimes he glanced up at the glaring sky, wishing to see the shadow of the Black Swan come to rescue him but another part of him remained curious. In the City there was so much to observe that was new and different. The streets were full of people busily going somewhere. The only ones who ever stopped were the old or the beggars. On all sides were houses and sometimes he glimpsed inside and saw families eating together or watching television.

"Don't you have a family?" one of the children asked him. "We all have, somewhere. Where do you come from?"

When the boy thought about that all he could see was the Garden in the curve of the sandy river. And when he told them about the fruit bats or the elephants rolling over in the shallows they said he was telling lies.

we all have families ...

The next day, when he was cooling off in the river, he met a schoolboy washing his bicycle. "What do you learn at school?" he asked him.   "I learn what I'm told," replied the boy with a laugh.

"I know that without going to school," said the boy, asking, "Do you learn to mend broken things?" The schoolboy shook his head.

"Do you learn how to make money?"   "No," said the boy.

"Do you learn to ... " he was about to say 'fly' but stopped, and when the schoolboy looked puzzled, asked "So what did you learn today?"

The schoolboy's face brightened. "From 7-8 I learned our language. From 8-9 arithmetic. From 9-10 our history, and from 10-11 another language."

"What other language?" asked the boy.

"Other people speak things in other ways," said the schoolboy, "And you must learn it to speak to them. Look at that foreigner over there."

what did you learn today?

The boy saw a tall, fair-haired man taking photographs. "He's a tourist," said the schoolboy. "He's come from far away to see the City. He speaks another language." And as if to explain the schoolboy smiled at the tourist and spoke haltingly to him.

"What was all that about?" asked the boy.

"I said 'Hello. How are you?' " explained the student.

Suddenly the boy exclaimed "He came in an aeroplane — ask him if he can fly!"

But the schoolboy snapped back angrily, "Of course not, you stupid gutter boy."

"If I could fly an aeroplane," thought the boy with sad longing, "I could soar above the City just like the Black Swan and I could find my way back to the Garden."

Just then he almost bumped into an old man in a monk's robe stepping very slowly along with his head bowed.

if only ...

"Have you lost something?" asked the boy.

The elderly monk regarded him steadily. "Everything I lost has no value. It is of no importance."

"Then what are you looking for?"

The monk smiled, "I am seeking enlightenment — the way and the truth," he added. "The truth that will enter into and lighten the soul. The truth that makes us whole."

The boy studied him anxiously. "You mean you are not whole? Are you ill?"

The monk smiled. "The body is well enough. I am seeking for the sake of my soul. Unless we can find enlightenment we are all trapped to the eternal wheel of life and death and rebirth."

The boy considered this gravely.

The monk went on: "Before you were born you have already lived a million lives. In each one by your own acts you improve slowly, gaining enlightenment, which will free you forever."

we've lived a million lives ...

"And if I do bad things?"

The monk shook his head. "Then you will pay for that in the next life. The rich greedy man may be reborn a beggar and the generous beggar a prince." The monk smiled. As they sat on the riverbank watching the boats being rowed along the monk remarked, "Our Guru — 'the Enlightened One', first sought enlightenment by fasting — denying His body and Himself everything. But He did not discover enlightenment."

"One day He watched a boat passing down river. In the boat a musician was teaching his pupil to play the guitar. Our Guru heard him say 'If you stretch the string too tight it will snap. If you loosen it too much it won't play.' At that moment our teacher realised it didn't matter to fast or not to fast but to walk and live a middle path between all extremes."

if the string is too tight ...

The monk produced a small food bowl from his robes. "After the musician left our Guru placed His food bowl on the stream. 'If I may find enlightenment,' He prayed, 'let this bowl float upstream.' "

The boy looked at him, questioningly. The monk nodded, "And it did."

After that the boy didn't mind being a garbage boy and he didn't mind begging but he always remembered to press his hands together and bow in thanks.

Learning

One morning near the market the boy met a man selling wood. He looked very poor. His clothes were full of holes and he was barefoot. He was selling bundles of firewood tied on the back of a broken-down bicycle. The man seemed cheerful and unworried.

"You look very poor," said the boy, concerned.

I'm not poor ...

"I'm not poor," exclaimed the man indignantly. "I have a lovely wife and 13 children. I'm not poor!"

The boy looked puzzled. "And you earn enough to buy them all food?"

The man nodded, "Just enough. But I'm not poor. I'll tell you what being poor is. Being poor is not having a wife, and not having children."

"Being poor is to be sick, or lonely or sad because someone you love has died or gone away. I have a good wife and 13 wonderful children." He pointed to a passing limousine and told the boy "those people may think they are rich — but in many ways they are poorer than I am with all their worries and problems." He dusted his ragged clothes and sat down beside his bicycle. "No, I'm not poor," he replied.

the best meal ever ...

He invited the boy to eat with him. He had only some stale rice and water but he shared this with as much ceremony as if it was a great feast.

Afterwards the boy thanked him, bowed and told him with total sincerity, "That was the nicest meal I've had."

The yard man, who was looking on, beckoned the boy. "Tonight you come and eat with me."

The boy was puzzled, for the yard man was very mean.

That same evening the yard man gave him yesterday's rice, crusts and water. Unlike the wood seller the boy knew the yard man gave him this food just to save money. "That's the worst meal I have ever eaten," he said truthfully.

The yard man became angry. "It was the same meal you had with the wood seller and you thanked him."

The boy just shook his head. How could he begin to explain the difference if the man did not know himself. "For the wood seller it was the most he could offer. For you it was the least," he told him.

walk and run?

At least if the boy was poor he could still feel thankful that he could walk and run, see and swim. For in that City there were thousands of young and old who were blinded and maimed by a war that was raging outside the City — and every day came a little closer.

It was not only soldiers who were wounded but country people ploughing their fields who stepped on landmines, or children walking to school or mothers collecting firewood, boys cutting bamboo.

A boy without hands or eyes sat by the Royal Pagoda of the King each day, begging. He explained to the boy how he had bent down to cut bamboo and something went bang and since then his world was black as night. And the boy felt tears start in his own eyes — for even sadder was to see the empty bloodied sockets in the child's face where not even tears could flow.

no eyes, no tears?

Later that day he returned to the pagoda with food to share with the boy, but he was not there.

"They take him away each night," he was told.

'They' were not his parents, but traders who bought maimed children and put them out each day to get money by begging.

The boy felt very sad; he carried his food to the river bank but felt too unhappy to eat. In the dusk he heard the beating of wings and looking up saw the shadow of the Black Swan landing beside him. "Do you want to go back to the Garden? Have you seen enough?"

The boy lay his head on the downy breast of the Swan. He said to the Swan, "But there are thousands and thousands who have no one to comfort them. No one to fly them back to the Garden. If I go away now I will always take the memory of their suffering with me. And I will never feel free as I was before."

have you seen enough?

"Now less than ever will I be able to fly. The City is like a dead weight dragging me down. It's not just the suffering but the filth, the noise, the greed, the hunger, the injustice, the anger, the lack of concern ..." The boy's voice trailed off wearily.

The Black Swan covered the boy's defenceless head with the shadow of his wing and spoke.

"Once long ago everyone lived in the Garden but people took it all for granted and started to abuse it. They chopped the trees and ate the animals and killed or imprisoned anyone who disagreed with them. They behaved as if they owned the Garden when really they were just guests like everything else. One day they decided they were every bit as clever as God and agreed among themselves to take over the Garden completely.

AMHERSTIA
Nobilis

God's favourite tree ...

"In the middle of the Garden there was a favourite tree God had planted and ordered no one to ever touch. The leaders of the people made everyone very excited with wild speeches and an unruly mob marched to the tree, cheering wildly, and chopped it down.

"They had thought they could be as wise as God but instead they argued and fought and behaved worse than ever. God decided to get rid of them all by causing a great flood to wash the Garden free of them. Before He did this He decided to share His plan with the only good man left.

"He instructed him to build a great raft and put on board two of every plant and animal living in the Garden, so that when the flood came they would be saved and that afterwards the Garden could be made again. Of course the man's neighbours all laughed at him for building this huge raft. Later when the rains poured down in a never-ending deluge their laughter fell silent.

all aboard?

"They watched in despair as the river burst its banks and floods swept over the Garden drowning everything and everyone. Now the people begged and pleaded to be allowed on board the floating raft. But God's resolve was not shaken and the raft sailed away without them. However, their cries and suffering so touched the heart of God that He decided no matter what crimes mankind committed in the future He would never interfere again.

"Instead He would send messengers and prophets and teachers to try and persuade the human race how it should live with itself. When the floods subsided God knew that although He would create another Garden in the curve of the great sandy river, man alone would be forbidden to enter. But He made a promise that they could return to it one day."

Keep Out!

The boy fell asleep and dreamed he was back in the Garden, lying in the cool shade beside the river and the Black Swan was fanning him gently with his wing as he spoke to him.

"The trouble was," the Black Swan continued in the boy's dream, "the people kept forgetting or ignoring God. Once, God chose a particular man to be their leader.

"He led them through the wilderness — through deserts and mountains, through famines and plagues — all with the one purpose of purifying them so they could return to the Garden. God even wrote down His laws on tablets of stone and gave them to this leader to show the people so they could have no excuse to ever forget again. This leader was very close to God! Each day he climbed to the mountain top to receive God's instructions. One day he asked to see God with his own eyes.

God passed by ...

"God replied, 'Not even you, my chosen friend, can see me. But if you hide behind a rock and keep your eyes shut tight I will pass close by and you can feel my Glory.' So the man did as he was told and God passed by. It was like a mighty rushing wind."

In his dream the boy looked up at the Swan. "Is that what God is like?"

"God is like everything and nothing," said the Swan. "One man asked if God is to be found in the heart of the hurricane or in the fiery inferno of a volcano, in the roar of thunder or the flash of lightning. 'No,' said God, 'Look for me in the still small voice of calm.' "

serenity ...

"A prophet," continued the Black Swan quietly, "promised God would come Himself. He claimed that the Spirit of God would be born in an ordinary human child who would later call Himself the Son of God. He would assume the responsibility of Saviour of mankind. He would comfort the poor and cure the sick and perform many miracles in God's name. He would show the true path to God. But in the end the authorities, especially the clergy, fearing His popularity and stung by His criticism, would turn the people against Him and put Him to death."

"But how can God die?" objected the boy.

"He came from God and by willingly giving up His human life, by allowing Himself to be tortured and die in disgrace He could offer His own life back to God as the only sacrifice perfect enough to forgive the sins and save the souls of all people. It was as if His dying was a ransom to pay for all the wrongdoings of mankind.

my life for theirs?

And because God would raise Him from the dead, He could offer the hope and promise of eternal life to everyone."

"And this prophet knew all this would happen?"

The Swan smiled, "He knew that the Son of God would be a living witness of the love and light of God freely given to all people.

"But this prophet also knew that most people expected God to arrive in a blaze of majesty and glory as if He was a great king, not as an ordinary human being."

"And did He ever come?" asked the boy, "or is it all just a story?"

But the Swan had vanished and the boy fell back asleep in the Garden of his dreams.

a haven of dreams

When he woke up he found the Swan had left him a message. "Hope is NOT something you can see, you have to wait for it. There is Faith, Hope and Trust but the one to cling to when all else is lost is Faith."

The boy wasn't sure this message comforted him very much. He shouldered his sack and went off to find refuse. When he saw a foreign lady carrying a plastic bag of rubbish he followed because he expected to find useful things: bent spoons, empty cans, broken shoes, torn clothes, bottles, uneaten food.

After the foreigner tossed her bag on the heap she watched the boy carefully scavenging and gave him a coin. "Thank you," bowed the boy. He noticed the foreigner rode an old bicycle with a number painted on it. Now most foreigners drove white jeeps or large motorbikes. "Why do you ride a bicycle?" enquired the boy.

"Because I can go slower," smiled the lady.

slow but sure ...

"You could walk," suggested the boy.

The lady shrugged and indicated the sun, "Walking is hot and I get tired."

"It's an old bicycle and very dirty," commented the boy.

The lady nodded. She surveyed the barefoot grubby boy standing knee deep in the garbage heap. "It's not what it looks like that matters, it's if it works well."

She added with a twinkle, "A bicycle is like a boy. He may be all shiny and clean on the outside but bad and lazy within or he may be dirty like you but good inside." The boy laughed and felt immediately better than he had all morning.

"Where are you going on your bicycle?" he asked her.

The lady indicated the row of numbers, "I rent it and each week I go to pay for it." The boy was puzzled, for a bicycle was not so expensive you had to rent it.

just passing through ...

"I like to rent," the lady explained. "I don't want to pretend I actually possess anything."

The boy frowned. "What about your clothes? Do you rent them?"

The lady laughed, "I just wear them out and then I can pass them on. You see we don't own anything in this life. It's a mistake to think of *my* this, *my* that. We're all just passing through." She thought for a moment.

"You may not realise it but you are luckier than most. You have fewer things to worry about."

"But I worry about what I don't have," argued the boy, closing his sack.

"Yes," agreed the woman, "but the more we have, the more we want. We're never satisfied. And the more you have the harder it is to get rid of. I stop myself when I see something I want and ask, But do I NEED it? I may want it, but do I need it? There's an awful lot we don't really need."

which way to turn?

"Do you need your bicycle?" teased the boy.

The woman grinned as she rode off. "Yes, I do," she insisted, but without conviction. But her smile remained long after she had gone and stayed to cheer the boy up.

Every day, working and walking bareheaded beneath the burning sun the boy's skin tanned dark brown.

The other children laughed. "You'll soon turn black," they teased.

"Oh, I don't think so," said the boy.

Then one day he met a man who was far darker. "Gosh, you are dark," he remarked. "I'm a black man," said the man.

"Not black, just dark brown."

"No, black," insisted the dark man.

"Then what am I?" asked the boy peering at his own skin.

"You are white, which means your are better, superior to me."

black or white

"But why — just because I'm not so brown?"

"Think about it," suggested the black man. "The light side of life — fun, gaiety; the dark side — pain, misery. Day and night, Heaven and Hell, white and black."

The boy couldn't accept this. "Why can't we all just be called brown?" he argued. "We are all brown after all, some light, some dark."

"The world don't work that way, son," confided the dark man. "And we've got to live in the world. In this world you are either black or white. It's decided the moment you are born. There's no in-between. You see," he continued, "although what we have in common is much more than what is different, people want to dwell on the differences. They feel safe set apart, so each group can learn to love to hate the other group. It makes them feel united and superior. I've just made you feel superior. I've told you you're a white fellow. You ain't at the bottom of the heap no more."

escape?

"But if you're a rich black man, driving a fine car with a big house ..."

"Don't make no difference," interrupted the black man. "Deep inside, nearly every black man is trying to escape into a white man by pretending he can be and act like a white man."

The boy thought of the Black Swan and how magnificent it looked when it flew and he remembered what the Swan had told him about darkness.

"It's what's in your soul that makes us dark or light," he told the man, "your soul and my soul ..."

The black man smiled and patted him. "There you are right. Souls are kindred spirits. Outside doesn't make no difference to the soul. It's the soul that draws us to God. It's on the wings of the soul that we will fly to God. It's the soul goes marching on — not the body." He saluted the boy and went on his way.

souls go marching on ...

One day as he toured the street with a bigger companion they came on a row of gaily painted wooden huts fronting a muddy alley near the river. Pretty girls sat outside making themselves up and gossiping, while small infants rolled about on the ground. The girls winked playfully at men passing by. A man stepped inside and at once a pink hospital screen was placed to shield him from view.

His companion tugged the boy's arm. "Follow me," he said and scampered round to the back of the hut. The plank wall was thin and full of cracks. The boys listened in silence. After a while the boy whispered, "What are they doing in there?"

"Making love," said his friend, "or pretending to."

"They seem to be making a lot of noise," remarked the boy. "It's how you get babies," his companion informed him afterwards.

fun for some?

"Was that what they were doing then?" asked the boy.

"No — they don't want babies. They were just enjoying themselves." He made a crude gesture with his hands. "That's having a good time. When you love someone you want to do it to them."

"Did they love each other?" asked the boy innocently.

"No, of course not," his friend laughed. "They were just pretending to for a short time."

"Both pretending?" enquired the boy.

"He was probably pretending more than she was. He pays her to pretend."

"Is it very costly to pretend this?" asked the boy.

"I think it can be." But his friend didn't know for sure. "Anyway the more beautiful the girl, the more she costs."

"And is the pretending any better?"

"I suppose so," his companion said. "But I've never had the money to try."

love or money?

It seems a great mystery, thought the boy as he made his way to the river to swim. At the bank he met the old monk. "I met a brown man who claimed he was black but whose soul was white and would fly to God one day," he told him.

"God is a mystery," said the monk. "Beyond everything made or created, that is or was, lies the Ultimate Mystery."

"There are lots of smaller mysteries," the boy said. "What I saw just now was a mystery."

"What was that?"

"I saw two people who were pretending to be making love and paying for it. It all seemed a mystery to me."

"The more they can keep it a mystery the longer the pretence can last," said the monk.

"Is God like that?" said the boy, thinking of the Black Swan. "Will God exist only if I pretend He is?"

"No, God will exist whether you or I pretend or not. God is the ultimate and sacred mystery: unborn, uncreated, unknown, the creator, the knower."

searching for God ...

"I know I was born," said the boy, "but I do not know very much about anything."

"You are not expected to," said the monk kindly. "You will not discover God trying to be wise or clever. After all no one can ever know the knower. God is a mystery and you will only come close to Him by sharing the mystery and entering the mystery. God is a bit like the City," he added wistfully.

"You think you know it and suddenly one day you see it in quite a different way. God has so many faces. God is spirit and if we seek Him we must seek Him in spirit and in truth. We cannot discover Him by knowledge or reasoning or science or technology, because God is the inspiration behind all science and all knowledge."

"People do so like to worship Gods," the monk sighed, "but so often they are worshipping their own wishful thinking. Our Guru did not want the responsibility for how men behaved to depend on any supreme being but on people themselves."

wings so vast ...

"If I think of a supreme being," mused the boy, "I think of the Black Swan and his wings so vast they enfold the entire world."

"But the Godhead," corrected the monk, "is not any supreme *being*. The Ultimate Mystery is unbeing, not made or created but from which everything is made and created."

Looking

One day the boy found himself outside what appeared to be a prison except that each cage contained different animals. "Why have they put you in these cages?" he asked, looking for a way to set them free. "Have you all done something very bad?"

"No, no," they assured him.

"We are here for our own protection."

animal prison?

"So that people can come and admire us."

"But you are all in a prison," said the boy.

"You see," explained a pink flamingo, "We are the very last of our race. If we escape and die, who will remember us?"

The boy immediately wanted to tell them about the Garden, but he thought it might only make them unhappy.

"People come to see me roar and growl," said the caged tiger. "And when I roar and growl it makes them happy."

"The children draw pictures of me," said the elephant, a heavy iron chain wrapped round his leg, "and climb on my back for rides."

"They all say how human I look" said the orangutan, "And want to have their photos taken beside me."

just like us

"Do you know our names?" they asked the boy. "They gave us each a name," roared the lion. "My name," added the orangutan, "means 'people of the forest' — what is a forest?" he asked the boy, through the bars of his cage.

"A forest is trees," the boy started to explain.

The animals nodded thoughtfully. "What is a tree?" asked a monkey cheekily.

So the more the boy tried to tell them about the forest the harder it became. They listened politely but it soon became obvious they disbelieved him.

"Sometimes we have dreams like that," a very large fish told him, mouthing the words through a glass tank, "but my memory is so poor I can never remember them."

love?

Not far from the zoo, near where an old wooden ferry chugged across the river, crowded with women carrying vegetables to sell in the market, there rose a steep isolated hill. An ancient temple capped this hill and people came to light candles and make offerings and pray to the spirits of their ancestors. Beggars and the maimed and crippled lined the steps rising to the temple and they were invariably rewarded.

The boy and his friends often passed this way and they also benefited from the impulsive generosity of those who hoped their prayers would be answered.

"What do they pray for?" asked the boy.

please ...

"Why, for good luck and good health. A winning lottery ticket and unexpected wealth," said the boys. "Don't you have anyone to pray to?"

"Yes, of course," the boy answered but he did not want to tell them of the Black Swan. Sometimes the Garden seemed so remote and far away he wondered if he had just imagined it, and it had existed only in his dreams and the City was the only reality.

As the boy struggled back, weighed down with his thoughts as much as his heavy sack, he recognised a familiar figure coming towards him. It was the foreign lady, but this time she was walking. The woman grinned, "You were right. I do not *need* a bicycle." And the smile they shared stayed with him all the way down the long and dusty road.

monsoon

So far the weather had been very hot but now dark clouds blotted out the sky.

Rain fell in a daily deluge that turned the streets into rivers and the rivers into raging torrents that finally burst their banks, flooding all the low-lying land and making many families homeless.

Using bamboo and banana stems they lashed together makeshift rafts to float off household possessions and live-stock to temporary shelters on higher land. But even the homeless accepted their plight quite cheerfully. As for the City — the whole population flocked to the riverside to swim and gambol in the rain.

moving house

Usually the downpours came in mid-afternoon and towards evening the skies cleared and the food sellers arrived in cyclos and spread out mats and small charcoal stoves. One of the most popular snacks was duck eggs ready-to-hatch. This delicacy was swallowed at a gulp — feathers and all. Children dived into the flooded river from trees and off the steps of the Royal Pavilion. Once in the water a total equality reigned. Once stripped off it made no difference who you were or what your background was.

All the children, rich and poor alike, enjoyed themselves together. The City was sited where two rivers met.
The bigger river flowed onwards to the sea but the smaller
river came out of a shallow inland lake a hundred miles
upstream. At this season the surge of water in the big river
pushed upstream into the smaller tributary and re-filled
the inland lake.

? ...

The boy didn't know the reason for it. He just watched
in amazement one day as the river started flowing back-
wards. It flowed very fast and when he swam, as he was
carried along, he remembered the monk's story of the Guru.
"If I may find enlightenment let this bowl flow upstream."

"Will I ever find enlightenment?" he wondered. "And
what will that be like?"

Listening

The war that had been raging outside the City grew
closer and sometimes they could hear the sound of gunfire
and explosions. One of the immediate results was that more
and more refugees crowded into the City and shanty towns
of thatch and plastic and cardboard grew up along the
swamps and the river banks.

cut ...

From time to time — usually when some important visitor
from overseas was coming, or an international meeting was
due to take place — the police arrived in force and tore
down the huts and herded the refugees away in trucks. On
these occasions the beggars and garbage boys kept out
of sight, but one day the boy unexpectedly found himself in
the middle of a violent demonstration.

Confronting the armed police and pelting them with stones stood a crowd of desperate people the police were trying to evict from their shacks.

The boy was astonished to see his friend, the foreign lady, in their midst. She took him aside. She was very angry. "It's disgraceful — all these people's homes are being torn down to make way for a floating Casino — where the rich can gamble their money."

stop!

Near them stood a man wearing what had once been a smart suit. "He looks like one gambler who lost," said his foreign friend. The man overheard and shook his head.

"Did you lose your job?" asked the boy sympathetically.

The man nodded, "I was a bank manager but I lost faith in money." The banker peered at the boy. "Do you know what a bank is?"

"It's where rich people put their money."

"Exactly! And all day long like a river money flows in and money flows out. Figures, lists, graphs, float like weeds in this river of money. Only you have to believe in it."

money? ...

"So long as you believe in the system you swim, but the moment you stop believing you sink."

"And you didn't believe in it?"

"Of course I did at first. Why, as a young man in the bank I was all bright-eyed and eager and raring to go. But when you handle thousands and thousands of Dollars and Francs and Ringits and Pounds and Marks and Lire and Baht and Pesos and ... Why, money starts to lose its appeal. It stops meaning anything.

"After all it wasn't my money and I never took it out of the bank. I began to question the whole value and notion of money. All these deposits people spend their whole lives saving and will never spend when they're dead. I began to tell customers that what they should be investing in was the next life. Gilt-edged securities of the soul, not the Government Treasury."

securities of the soul

He made a wry grin. "Of course they thought I was just crazy, but my boss knew I was dangerous. You see, the Capitalist system only works, only keeps roaring ahead as long as everyone believes in it. The system relies on confidence and conviction. Once this gets punctured — why, the whole caboodle can collapse overnight.

"Capitalism is only a bright shining bubble — pop it and it bursts into nothing. International financiers juggle currencies like baubles for profit when these same currencies are the bedrock of a nation and assure the livelihood of millions of people. The whole system is founded on the rotten idea that greed and gain are good. The only capital that counts is what you store in your heart not in the bank."

"What will you do now?"

what is wealth?

"I am waiting for the revolution to come," he said placidly. "They tell me these rebels don't believe in money either. They say they're going to do away with it altogether and put everyone back to planting rice. It sure makes sense to me."

The foreigner who had been arguing with the police came back bloodied and bruised with her blouse torn. "They have no respect for human rights," she complained bitterly. "No respect at all."

"What are human rights?" asked the boy, but the foreign lady was too busy handing out money and medicine to the distraught people whose huts had been burned or town down to reply.

human rights?

Later she took the boy aside. "Every human being has rights," she told him, " — the right to some sort of house, however simple; the right to get water, to work, to live without harassment — it's not asking much, is it? And it's the responsibility of a government to help the people to obtain their rights. They should be protecting these people."

"The government is just the big boss," said the boy. "Why should it listen to anyone?"

"A government is meant to be there to serve the needs of the people — not just to get rich themselves. You want something here — then you buy the politician. Somebody wants to bring a casino here — even though gambling is officially 'illegal.' It means nothing that people live here. Or even pay annual taxes for their shanty huts — these are bulldozed away like dirt. And, if they object, or don't go or protest ... " she slid a finger under her throat.

lucky for some

Then she shrugged. "But they say I'm just an interfering foreigner. They say these people are used to this system, and wouldn't understand democracy. And you know what democracy means here — vote buying."

"What is a vote?" enquired the boy.   "A vote is your choice. In democracy every adult, rich or poor, has a choice. But some are scared to use it, others don't care and some sell their choice to people who want to be chosen to govern and who buy as many votes as they can."

"So the wealthy ones get chosen?"   The woman nodded. "They have to get their money back so they do all sorts of corrupt things. Businessmen have to pay them to get contracts; so does anyone else who wants their help.

PARTY		VOTES CAST	
GET RICH	😵 $	|||| |||| |||| |||| |||	✓
STAY RICH	😐	|||| |||| ||	✗
NO CORRUPTION	😊	|||	✗

what's it worth?

"Where I come from everyone has the right to an education, free access to hospitals, money if they can't find work, and the right to a pension when they are old. But I daren't tell people that here."

"Nobody would believe you if you did."   The woman laughed. "The funny thing is over there everyone takes it for granted. They complain far more *there* than they do here. Over there they think they are badly off if they can't afford a new car." Once again she and the boy shared a laugh together and felt the better for it.

The question of human rights seemed to be about to answer itself when the boy passed a deserted-looking building with a peeling board outside announcing "Office for Protection of Human Rights."

is this for me?

There was certainly plenty of waste paper and crumpled leaflets in the bins, but no one to question what it all meant.

Finally he saw a man emerge and asked him.

"Don't worry yourself," he assured the boy. "It's got nothing to do with you." The City was full of similar buildings with similar foreign-sounding names.

Red Cross, World Vision, Save the Children, War on Want. There were usually large white jeeps in the courtyards and security guards to 'shoo' anyone away. Sometimes he saw the jeeps with their bright emblems and flags roaring along the streets but nobody seemed to know where they were going. When the boy asked he always got the same answer: "It's some foreign thing."

saving the world?

"They have nothing to do with us."

Often in the early evening the boy came across the foreign lady — only now she was back on her bicycle. "I really *do* NEED it!" she cried breathlessly. The front basket was filled with packets of steaming rice and hard boiled eggs and bananas, which she was handing out to homeless people or hungry children.

"Phew!" she said, mopping her brow. "Sometimes I think if the bicycle was edible they'd eat that too!" She always carried a big first aid tin which seemed to contain a little of everything: headache pills, cures for diarrhoea, creams to heal rashes, tablets to stop fever and toothaches, even fillings for cavities. "I'm a 'band-aid' girl," she told the boy. "A lady bush doctor: Bible, band-aids and bicycle."

"What's a bible?" asked the boy.

between the lines?

The lady smiled. "It's a book that helps me on my journey. Lots of good things in it," she added a bit mysteriously. "Can you read?" she asked the boy.

"Just a bit. The big letters," the boy smiled.

"Then at least you can't read between the lines," laughed the lady.

This puzzled the boy and when he next got hold of newspaper he tried hard peering between the lines of print but gained nothing except an eye-ache.

If street people got sick they just lay there till they got better. There were old women who knew about healing. They didn't use the tablets or lotions of the foreigners, they believed in thrashing with a branch. Across the chest — if you had a cough. The thrashing brought the blood to the surface and helped the circulation; or there were hot suction cups applied to the skin to draw out the pain. Only the rich people went to doctors. "And they usually choose an old one," someone explained. "The older ones have already learned by their mistakes on earlier victims."

street surgery

Doctors handed patients letters for shops that sold medicine, but ordinary people didn't trust the pills and potions, as they doubted what was in them. Often — so it was rumoured — they were nothing more than flour and sugar.

Sometimes in the evening the people of the street were entertained by actors who set up a stage and dressed in fancy costumes, danced and sang and told stories. Always they were dressed up in costumes no one wore any more and the stories were of olden times — of heroes and villains and tragic romances.

street theatre

There were other theatres for rich people — but these were out of sight and you had to pay to go in.

One day the boy, who was collecting bottles outside the stage door, met one of the players. Unlike the friendly street actors this one seemed rather stuck up. He was practising his lines.

"Each week," he explained loftily, "I have to learn my part for the next week's play." "Don't you ever get muddled up?" asked the boy.

"Of course not," snapped the actor. "After all I'm a professional. It's my job to pretend to be someone I'm not." The boy looked confused. "Why?"

"A play," explained the actor, "is a copy of life, but all condensed into a couple of hours — dramas, murders, love. Art copies life," he pronounced with authority.

art copies life?

"Why do you need to copy life?" asked the boy. "I should have thought you'd want to escape from it."

"Of course it does that too," agreed the actor. "In the theatre are the actors and the audience. The actors enable the audience to identify and explore their emotions. Oh, how they laugh or cry at our performances! A well-acted play brings out their finest feelings. They can get back into their lives like new people."

The boy was puzzled. "But does it help them for long? Most of the people I seem to see coming out of theatres are the same people who went in."

"The theatre is not supposed to be a religion," said the actor huffily. "It's only an illusion after all. A bit of a trick."

coming or going?

"But if it's supposed to copy life then life must be an illusion too!" protested the boy.

The actor snorted indignantly. "I haven't the time to bandy words with garbage boys!" he declared. "I have to learn my lines. Next week I have a very important part. I am a lawyer — I have to impress everyone with my cunning." He glared at the boy with lowered eyelids.

When he went to the river the boy met a man carrying a large folding easel and a box of paints, blank canvasses, tubes, rags and bottles. He seemed on the point of dropping things and as the boy's sack was still half empty he helped the painter with his load.

stealing the light

"What are you doing?" he asked as the painter set up his easel on the riverbank and squirted paints onto his palette. "Are you copying life like the actor?"

"No," smiled the painter. "I am a thief." He winked at the boy.

"A thief?" repeated the boy, startled and backing away.

The painter laughed. "I steal light! Now, look over there."
He guided the boy's hand and pointed to where the late
afternoon sunlight was glowing from beneath the lowering
clouds. The glow spread to the golden roofs of the royal pagoda. The painter sighed. "That is what I want to capture,
to put down the light." He shook his head.

a word of God

His silver hair and grey moustache all glowed in the
reflected light but the canvas remained blank.

"Aren't you going to paint anything?" the boy suggested
after a while.

The old painter spread wide his arms. "Sometimes I am
just so amazed at the beauty of light," he said, "I just want
to share its mystery. Light," he said majestically, "is a gift of
God, a word of God. A whole language like silence."

"Like the sky," said the boy thinking of the Swan.

"And the light shines in the darkness and the darkness doesn't understand," added the painter softly.

"What is that?" asked the boy.

"It comes from an old book — written a long time ago," said the painter, "but the line I like best is: 'God is Light. In Him is no darkness at all.' "

God is Light

"Light doesn't just come from the sun," he told the boy, "Light shines from the love of God." He pinched together his fingers as if to trap a glimmer. "And a little of that light glows in each one of us. If we let it."

"You are not a painter. You are a priest," said the boy.

"No," said the painter with a laugh. "I am a thief of light, but not a very successful one."

The full moon towards the end of the year marked the festival of 'candle floats.' The day of the festival was busy with preparations, and towards evening everyone carried their floats to the river bank. The breeze died with the sunset. The air stilled, and as the full moon rose above the darkening river the candle-lit floats were set gently on the water's edge and drifted slowly out into the stream.

pray for peace

The boy met his friend, the elderly monk, who was gazing placidly at the scene. "Why?" asked the boy. "Why?" replied the monk. "When you peer into a candle flame don't you wish or dream?" The boy nodded. "Everyone is aware of their own frailties," remarked the monk, watching the river now invaded by thousands of flickering candles. "We get comfort from these gestures we make together, sharing our hopes and fears." "But if the candles go out?" asked the boy, anxiously following his own float, "does that mean our dreams will die too?" The monk smiled. "The sun goes out, but tomorrow still comes." "Then what should I pray for?" asked the boy, thinking only of the Black Swan and the Garden. "Pray for peace," the monk suggested.

Shortly after the festival of candles, the annual kite flying began. This wasn't just for children — everyone joined in. Most people made their own kites. Sidewalks and table-tops were strewn with coloured paper, glue, sticks and string. Street vendors did a brisk trade. The poorer children cut out plastic bags or newspapers. Day by day the afternoon sky filled with kites of every shape and size. Looking like birds and bats, dragons and owls, they swooped and darted, soared and plunged, to the accompaniment of shrieks and laughter and howls of glee.

soaring aloft

Judging by the cluster of kites rising above the pagodas, even the young monks joined in the sport. The old monk shaded his eyes to watch. "Are these like our dreams, too?" the boy asked him, thinking of the floating candles. "Perhaps they are," nodded the monk, "but I think it's rather as if our spirits were soaring with them." He smiled. "Look around — do you see any glum faces?"

As the boy craned his head back to scan the sky his delight was tempered only by a wistful longing to be up there too, flying high through the bright, thin air.

Leaving

These were strange days. The war, and noise and rumour of war was every day coming closer. People were streaming into the City or going out of the City in carts and bicycles, cars and buses loaded with possessions.

The boy met many people putting things together for their journey.

just keep going ...

He found a very old man standing undecided on a street corner.

"I don't know where to go," he told the boy. "All my life I have been seeking a secret haven."

The boy listened attentively. "You see, it does not matter how long the search takes, nor where it takes you," said the old man.

"In fact, when you set out, pray the road be long and the experiences many. Learn and learn again from those you meet on the road, but always keep your goal fixed in your mind. That is your ultimate aim, never be diverted from it. Better you take long years and arrive finally at the harbour in the evening and drop anchor as the moon is rising over the mountains." He gazed thoughtfully at the boy.

to anchor at evening

"And what if you should find the place a disappointment? Will your voyage have been all for nothing?"

He shook his head resolutely. "Not a bit of it. You see, without your ideal you would never have started out in the first place. This dream you had, why — it gave you the journey; and think, think how much you have gained on the way."

One day the boy met a very angry man tearing at his own hair. "I am always angry and I wish I wasn't," said the man unhappily. "Every day I try to remind myself not to be ill-tempered or irritable or unkind — I even write it down. But the slightest little thing sets me off, and although I know I should stop, I can't. I rage and roar and bellow and judge and condemn until the anger is all burned out and then I bitterly regret it. But a little while later I'm off again, and mostly to people I like, which makes it worse."

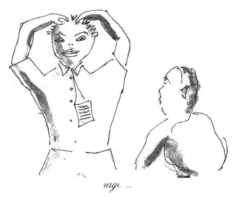

rage ...

"I've tried everything," he went on. "Change of diet, sleeping pills, alcohol, music, hypnosis. Nothing works. I am out of my own control. I pray that the anger will wash out and I'll be left free of it because I know it's pointless and I never remember afterwards what made me angry in the first place."

"Perhaps you should go and live at the temple with the monks," suggested the boy.

"I tried but I only got angry with them too — over nothing. I'm better off on my own — then I can only be angry with myself."

The angry man had a card hanging around his neck. "It's meant to remind me," the man said and recited, "Think deeply, speak gently, love much, laugh often, give freely, pray earnestly and be kind." He threw up his hands in despair. "I have all the rules," he declared, "but I can't keep one of them." He tugged a tattered book from his pocket and pointed to a page. He read aloud: "Love is patient and kind. It is not jealous or conceited or proud."

love is kind!

"It's not ill-mannered or selfish or irritable. Love does not keep a record of wrongs ..." He slammed a finger angrily on the page. "And I am always irritable and I never forget wrongs — in fact I dream of the most terrible revenge I could inflict. And I hate myself because I cannot stop. I hate it!" he stormed angrily, and strode away, red and fuming.

Near the market where the children ate a boy was leading a blind old man who was plucking at a single stringed violin and warbling a song all out of tune. The old blind musician sat down to eat with them. "An old man," he said suddenly, "is just a tattered coat upon a stick unless — " he peered at the boy with sightless eyes, "Unless his soul clap its hands and sing," he wheezed, raising his tinny voice, "and louder sing for every tatter in its mortal dress."

singing masters of the soul

"Is that what you are doing?" asked the boy.

The blind musician nodded confidentially. "I am going to find the singing masters of my soul. And get me to the Holy City."

"Where's that?"

"Oh, it's a dream, the dream I have been searching for all my life. But it's where my immortal soul belongs." He picked up his broken fiddle. "And if I ever put on mortal form again what do you think I might want?"

"To see," suggested the boy.

song of dreams

The blind man shook his head. "Oh, I can *see* now," he said. "No, I should like to be a palace bird, perched on a golden bough singing to all the lords and ladies about what was, and is, and is to come."

There was a hotel near the market where many young foreign travellers stopped. They came into the City with huge backpacks, hair long and clothes grimy, but they seemed to have no shortage of money when it came to eating or drinking beer. There was an open-air restaurant below the hotel where they all gathered to gossip.

thirsty work

Beggars and maimed soldiers came by, hats in hand, but these travellers were very mean when it came to giving anything away. The boy was looking into the video game parlour next door where the school kids were playing combat games on the screens with great enthusiasm. A man thrust a coin at the boy.

"Do you want to play? — Go on." The boy shook his head. "All the games are war games — just like all the films."

The man nodded. "That's what everyone seems to like. Violence is the way of the world." He was dressed like a traveller except he was older and didn't have the backpack, or the plastic bottle of drinking water or big dirty boots.

"What are you?" asked the boy politely.

"I'm an explorer," the man replied.

The boy studied him carefully. "You don't look like an explorer," he told him. "Shouldn't you have a big backpack with a tent and a compass and ropes and maps and things?"

explorers

"It all depends what you are going to explore," said the explorer. "If you are going to explore mountain passes you need ropes and ice picks and if you are going to cross deserts you need water and a compass."

"So what are you going to explore?"

The explorer glanced around uncertainly as if he had a secret he didn't want anyone to hear.

Overhead the moon had risen — a nearly full moon glowing in a cloudless night sky. The explorer pointed "There's a far side to the moon that no one has ever seen except the astronauts."

"That's where you're going?"

The explorer shook his head and pointed to the river — broad as a sea by night. "Centuries ago sailors set out from here to try and reach the other side of the world.

land ahoy!

"Everyone thought they were crazy because everyone knew that the world was flat and once you got to the edge you fell off."

"Is that where you are going?"

The man looked hard at him, "I'm setting off to discover the other side of the soul. You think I'm crazy?"

The boy merely frowned. "But how do you set off on such a journey and what do you take with you?"

"One thing I've learned," replied the explorer, "is when you give up anything it is as if you are setting out on a journey towards an unknown goal. But when you give up something, you always gain something else, although you won't know what until it happens."

"If I gave up collecting rubbish," said the boy, "I'd just go hungry." But the explorer was already away on the brink of his journeyings and didn't hear him. "Perhaps it is music you abandon, and cast yourself free into a seemingly silent world where the only sound is the wind sighing or the waves breaking." The explorer paused.

music of the spheres

"Perhaps when you are older and have had someone to love, you may realise that desire is an unreliable foundation for affection and decide to do without it. At first you will feel like a solitary hermit setting out into the unknown alone — but like every journey it will bring its rewards, however difficult it is to predict them. You see we have to set ourselves free and cast off all those things familiar to us if we are ever to discover what lies within us on the other side of our own soul."

He waved an arm gently around them. "This landscape outside, of rivers and fields and streets and houses, of work and play, is much the same wherever we go — as are the problems — but the landscape on the other side of the soul is unknown and there are few indeed who are prepared to break with their familiar ways and set out like an early explorer and not look back."

don't look back

He watched the traffic. "You cannot set out on this journey by car or motorbike or even a bicycle. Perhaps not even on foot. But you have to set off with intent and the pangs and the suffering and the wish to return to the familiar will be very hard to bear at the start. So ask yourself: do you have the strength and do you have the purpose? They will be your companions, and trust and faith will be your guides.

"We must believe that our soul, like our planet, is round and there is something on the other side. The temptation is to feel as uncertain as those early navigators, fearful if they went too far they would fall over the edge and plunge into the abyss. That is why all those things familiar to us and in which we take such pleasure have such a strong hold over us.

burn your boats!

"How hard it is for us to burn our boats so that we cannot return to the beckoning shore of our own cravings. But if we wish to discover a new dimension, if we wish to free ourselves from these bonds then we must close our ears and shut our eyes and strike out into the deep for the unknown shore of our own soul — wherever it may be."

Then the boy confided with the explorer and told him about the Garden. He told him everything, and the explorer listened patiently until he finished. "I have only one question to ask you," he said. "If there are two paths, the narrow stony path that leads to your Garden or the broad, well-lit comradely path of the satisfaction of your pleasures and desires, which one will you take?"

which way?

The boy hesitated, "I hope I would take the narrow path to the Garden — but it isn't clearly marked, is it?" he pleaded.

"No," agreed the explorer, "If it were, there would be no test of faith and hope. For what is seen cannot be hoped for. By faith we must seek this other country. For you the Garden, for me the gate of the soul. And we must trust ourselves to the path of hope to get there."

"What is the most important part of you?" he asked the boy. "The body you can see and feel — until it dies, or your soul, which you cannot see or feel but is the real you, and if you strengthen it, will fly through the open door of death, while the body, however richly you have sustained it, will fail and fall."

through an open door?

At Last

The war grew nearer. Rebels were said to be massing along the other side of the river — hiding in the rice fields waiting to launch their attack on the City. The backpackers and their fellow travellers began to desert the hotel and take to the ferries going down river. The police seemed more jittery than ever. Now they harassed everyone they could stop except the big dark-windowed limousines that might contain important people or high-ranking officers. But the cyclo drivers and motorcycle riders were constantly stopped and had to pay on-the-spot fines. Then the police started asking to see identity cards (which none of the street people possessed) and demanding money when they couldn't produce them.

just checking?

Some people continued about their business apparently unconcerned. Each day the boy had been watching a man building a simple two room house. "Are you building a shop?" asked the boy. "I am building the house of Life and Death," replied the builder rather sadly, and invited the boy to come and see. One room was already completed and furnished, the other room was empty and half-built. "That is death?" asked the boy, pointing to the empty room.

The builder shook his head gloomily. "The room full of my useless possessions is death. The empty room is life."

"I don't understand," said the boy.

"Just look around," said the man. "Everywhere you look one is persuaded to fill one's life with junk. One can cook just as well on three stones, but no, one must have a cooker. And it's not just material rubbish — the movies and magazines all make us believe our life is empty unless we fill it with romance and greed, lust and intrigue."

property rights ...

"We are so convinced by this propaganda that a life without such things seems an empty and lonely prospect. And because we clutter our life with such rubbish, death, which means the end of all those silly things, seems so negative and frightening. So we acquire more and more to help us pretend we are more secure." He chuckled. "It is like sand bags against a flood. However much we try to stop it, death will burst through in the end."

"Look at this room with all its trappings — many of them represent things you cannot recognise — but I do. They symbolise all the worst aspects of my life: cravings and desires, and self-importance. Although I keep meaning to throw them all out I never do." "So why don't you just move into the other room? There can't be any memories for you there."

"I have tried," the man sighed. "I have even tried locking the room of death and throwing away the key. But after a while my craving to go back, just for a glimpse, was too powerful to be endured and I broke the door down to get in."

I wish ...

"Then couldn't you make the life room more comfortable?" suggested the boy. The builder nodded, "Of course I could. Yes, indeed! I know exactly what I would put in it — I would fill it with kindness, self control, patience, compassion, generosity, joy — " he stopped, close to tears. "Only where can I obtain such things? I am like someone who wants to make music so much he buys the instrument, only to discover he cannot buy the skill to play it. If only there was a shop — an 'Emporium of the Soul.' "

"I have often imagined just such a shop." He closed his eyes and pressed his hands excitedly together. "When the door opens an old-fashioned bell tinkles and a little old lady, her hair primly in a bun and spectacles perched on the tip of her nose, comes in from the back. The dusty shelves are lined with jars labelled with everything the soul needs to be healthy."

come on in ...

"The little old lady measures out the amount of each you want — a little of this, a little of that." He made a deep sigh and his eyes opened. "But there is no shop — not even at the temple. Such things you have to make yourself and I am a poor craftsman."

"When I try to make them they fall to pieces at the first tremble of my real nature, the first murmur of impatience, the first snort of indignation — and all my best intentions vanish and the room is bare and empty as before."

As the boy left the builder was shaking his head over the house he could never complete.

That night the boy had the strangest dream. There in front of him stood an old-fashioned shop named 'Emporium of the Soul' and the door opened with a jingling bell and a little old lady with spectacles and hair in a bun came forward to serve him. "Do you have a bar of soap?" asked the boy. "My body is so dirty."

"No, no," the old lady shook her head. "This is not a shop for the body. Here you will find everything you need to satisfy your soul."

"But I can't see my soul," argued the boy.

The old lady suddenly transformed into the Black Swan. "But your soul can see you," said the Black Swan. "And perhaps it is sad when you neglect it."

where is it?

War

The attack started as predicted, across the river. The government soldiers were said to be surrendering en masse. After an initial flurry of activity the City seemed deserted. When the boy went to sell his cans he found the yard closed. The traders had gone. Suddenly around midday there were prolonged bursts of firing and a column of jubilant rebels entered the City crowded on jeeps and old trucks — shooting victoriously into the air.

deserted

The street people and garbage children joined in the celebrations but few others did. Most people stayed in their homes. There were no cars on the streets. Even the monks did not leave the temple.

Next day the people's fears were realised as the rebels announced through loudspeakers that everyone had to leave.

The entire population was ordered out of the City and no one was allowed to take more than they could carry.

"The City is corrupt," declared the rebels. "From now on there will be no city, no offices, no shops, no banks, no money, no temples, no schools, no television, no radio. *Everyone* will work on the land. Everyone will grow food."

all out!

Rebel soldiers moved into every street and searched every house in turn, making sure that no one was staying behind. As the people were herded out of the City they had to pass checkpoints where they were inspected. Anyone with clean soft hands joined a separate column. These included traders, shopkeepers, teachers, monks, judges, politicians, policemen, and doctors.

All these men and their wives and families were de-
tained in the compound of the City high school that was now
ringed by barbed wire and guarded by soldiers. "They are
kept for interrogation," ran the rumour darkly.

The boy and his companions joined the other procession
out of the City into the countryside.

guilty or not?

For most families these were very difficult days. The
rains had not ceased and the roads, destroyed by the war,
turned into muddy quagmires. Children cried, mothers
quickly exhausted their supplies of food. The armed guards
shot anyone picking food.

The villages they entered could not or would not help
them. Each day the suffering grew worse.

The street children, who were used to scavenging found it hard to scrape together enough to survive, but for others unused to rough living it was far worse. Old and young dropped by the roadside, collapsing from hunger or thirst, fever or diarrhoea. The armed guards showed no sympathy. Anyone who could not stay on their feet was clubbed to death or just left to die.

drop dead

At another place they were inspected again and the fitter ones taken aside.

"You will be a soldier," they were told.

"And you must trust no one. There are enemies of the revolution everywhere. Everyone who had anything to do with the old corrupt regime is a spy. Naturally for their own protection they will try to pretend they had nothing to do with it. They will claim they had humble jobs, but you will be able to catch them out, by the way they speak, the way they act."

"If you suspect anyone — even your close friend, your wife, your husband, your father, it is your duty to report them. It is your duty to betray your neighbour. Not to do this is to betray the cause and to betray yourself."

you're a soldier now

Instead of a sack of rubbish the boy now carried a gun. He still wore the same ragged clothing; torn T-shirt and shorts and broken flip-flops, but as a badge of his new role he had a red scarf tied round his head.

The new recruits were given basic training — which amounted to little more than learning how to clean and fire their rifles, throw a hand grenade, place a landmine.

Whenever they wanted to rest they had to listen to revolutionary propaganda about the evils of the City and the corrupt people who lived there. But the City seemed far off in his memory, and as for the Garden, it was like a dream, and he began to doubt it had ever existed.

lesson of war

Duty?

For a long time they had been fighting an enemy he had never seen. They lived in the jungle — but it was unlike the forest he still occasionally dreamed of. This jungle was full of terror. When they went along a path they never knew if death lurked around the next bend. When they crossed a clearing they never knew if they were stepping into a minefield.

mind your step

At the camp they slept on mats on the damp earth under simple stick and thatch shelters. The food was never more than a handful of sticky rice and a pinch of salt. Each day people were denounced as traitors and taken into the forest and bludgeoned to death.

One of the men at the camp befriended the boy and showed him how best to use and clean his weapons.
The boy was curious how he knew so much but the man made a wry grin.

"I wasn't someone you would want to meet very often when I lived in the City," he said.

"Why?" asked the boy, puzzled.

"I was the Chief Executioner," the man explained. "The job's been in the family for generations," he added proudly.

obey!

"In those days it was all beheadings and disembowelling," he said with a certain relish. "Nowadays, a lot cleaner — a pistol shot. Some days I've been that busy packing them off to paradise by the barrel load. We've had all sorts — the mighty and the not so mighty. They all get to be very humble when I come to call." He winked at the boy. "One of my ancestors even executed the Son of God!" He laughed at the boy's astonishment. "There's this legend that, long ago, God came to the City in disguise."

"Why?" asked the boy.   The executioner shrugged. "To try it out, I suppose. Just like everyone else. Everybody had been told to expect Him but when He finally came no one recognised Him."   "No one recognised God?" repeated the boy, startled. "Nobody?"   "You can't blame them entirely," said the executioner. "As no one had ever seen Him they could only imagine what He might look like."   "How did He arrive?" asked the boy.   The executioner scratched his cheek. "That's the joke. God's joke. He arrived like everyone else — born a baby." He guffawed, "And not in some palace but to a family of street people." The boy frowned. "Anyone can pretend to be someone he's not."

off with his head!

"Yes," agreed the executioner. "But it's what He did, you see. He cured the sick, fed the hungry, even turned water into wine, they say." The man licked his lips. "Told people to live as if God was inside them and to love their neighbour." "Anyone?" said the boy, astonished.   "Everyone, I suppose," said the man.   "Then why was He executed?"   "Rubbed too many important people the wrong way. Can't have the son of street people claiming to be the Son of God and knowing more about Him than all the priests put together."

"Mob popularity. The Government of the day felt threatened. Half my clients, one might say, are 'political.' 'Course He was innocent. No one denies that. The judge even called for a bowl of water and washed His hands of the verdict — before handing Him over to a rent-a-mob and my great grandfather. I don't suppose judges are any different nowadays. Do what they're told mostly. Anyway sometimes you have to sacrifice the good to save the bad."

"Why save the bad?" asked the boy. "I suppose the good are saved already. Anyway my grandfather did the business. Crucifixion it was called — nailing the client to a wooden cross and letting them hang. Very painful, I believe."

nailing!

The boy thought for a moment. "I expect He screamed and cursed His tormentors?"

"Not a bit of it," said the executioner. "Told everyone to love their enemies. Called on God to forgive His murderers. My grandfather was most impressed. 'Never met a client like Him before.' He came away convinced he had executed the Son of God. Never worked again. Handed the job over to his son and became a monk." The executioner chuckled. "Now let's not forget that rifle of yours — out here it's your best friend. Once you get me talking I'm hard to stop."

But he did stop soon after. For next morning one of the soldiers denounced the executioner as a 'persecutor of the poor' and a 'tool of the rich and powerful,' and he was led off to face the same fate he had handed out to so many before.

Life in the jungle was very hard. If you were too sick to work you were considered a traitor to the revolution.

don't slip!

Nearly everyone was sick with malaria and chronic dysentery but there were no medicines. One day one of the boy's friends from the City fell out of a high palm tree that he had climbed to cut coconuts. He lay writhing on the ground clutching his broken thigh.

They carried him to the hut and strapped up the leg as best they could. The injured boy lay on the floor groaning most of the night and by dawn he had a raging fever.

They wiped him down with wet cloths but they could not set the broken bone. Every time they tried to splint the leg the broken ends seemed to jerk free in spasm. Finally one end of the bone punctured the skin. Later the boy started to twitch and his jaw locked so they had to prise his mouth open to pour in water. His eyes had a haunted, scared look.

help me

The boy, who had been at his side since the accident, stepped out of the hut. Tall palm trees framed the clearing and above them fluffy white clouds swam in the clear blue sky. After the gloom of the hut the boy shielded his eyes against the bright sunlight. He felt resentful that this world of nature outside could be so detached and indifferent while in the hut his friend lay dying in agony.

At dusk the boy left the clearing alone, and kneeling in the forest, he prayed that the boy be healed. He prayed for the Black Swan to fly down and lift him away in his webbed feet and take him to the Garden and cure him. He prayed with such intense concentration he could feel drops of sweat pouring off his face. Never had he prayed so hard, or with such single-mindedness for anything or anyone.

help him

By now night had fallen and stars glittered in the jet black sky. The boy approached the hut hoping and hoping that a miracle had happened. But to his dismay the sick boy was worse. Spasms racked his body. Only his eyes stared at them in a desperate plea for help.

The boy knew the exact moment his friend had died, for in the night he was bitten on his elbow by a giant millipede and the sting was excruciatingly painful, especially as he couldn't reach the wound to suck it. It was as if the spirit of the dead boy had given him a nip as it flew away — a nip to remind him he had not tried hard enough to save him.

a timely nip?

The day the boy was buried they were ordered to attack their enemies, who were grouped in a nearby village. As they approached across muddy rice-fields, firing started and landmines exploded under them. The boy saw his friends shot or blown up one by one until they all lay limply as bundles of bloodstained rags in the rice fields.

After the firing stopped the boy pushed his way through the mud towards them but he knew they were all dead. And they were killed for what? The boy threw down his gun in disgust and walked away, back the way they had come. How he wished they could all go back — back to the life they had before.

rain or tears

The boy stood still, revolving many memories. Above him raindrops dripped from the trees as if grieving for his fallen comrades. But nature never grieves, he reflected bitterly. It was too busy with its own affairs to concern itself with mankind's problems. For a moment the callous indifference of nature made him resentful. He felt an urge to hit a tree — but stroked it instead. This pointless slaughter was not nature's fault. This waste came from man. His gaze passed slowly over the field of dead.

Is this what they had struggled for each day, collecting
in the City? Each one with their hopes and expectations.
To end up like this, lying in a field, their life drained out of them.
The boy could not have felt more alone and abandoned as
he set off slowly back towards the camp, not caring if he
arrived or not. In his mind he already saw — like a photograph
of fate — his own corpse lying in the mud.

that's me

That night the Black Swan came to him as in a dream.
"I have done terrible things," whimpered the boy through his
tears. "I deserve to be punished for I have failed."

But the Black Swan only drew his wing more tightly
around him. "Nothing outside you can make you unclean. It is
what is in you. The intention is more important than the act."

The Black Swan whispered, "The good I would, I do not," and then, holding the boy firmly he told him, "I am not wholly I, and you are not wholly you. But I am a part of you and you are part of me. And you will always find me and come to me through the part of me that is in you and I will always find you through the part of you that is in me."

please ...

"And remember —, neither death nor life, neither the present nor the future, neither good people nor bad, neither suffering nor joy, neither problems nor promises, neither anything near us nor far from us nor anything else in all creation can separate you and me and everyone else from the Love of God."

But when he awoke in the morning worse was to come. At the parade he was denounced by the boy next to him. "He is a monk," accused the boy. "He prays. I followed him and saw it and heard it."

"Monks are parasites!" screamed the commander. "Leeches living off the people, bloodsuckers living off superstition and myth — claiming the best food, the best seats, always claiming to be superior. Anyone who is a monk is a traitor to the revolution!"

traitor!

The boy was stripped of his red scarf and thrown into the back of a truck crammed with other so-called traitors, and driven back to the City, where they were unloaded and sent for interrogation at the high school near the temple.

The school was now barricaded with razor wire, and guardposts. Wire-netting covered the outside corridors on the upper levels, "To prevent anyone trying to throw themselves off!" a guard informed them grimly. Each classroom on the upper floor had been divided into tiny bricked-off cells six feet long and three feet wide where the prisoners were chained to the floor.

no hope

The rooms on the ground floor were used for interrogation and all day long the building echoed with the hideous cries and screams of people being slowly tortured. The boy was shown an interrogation room to frighten him. The guards were washing out remains of blood and gore. There were pincers for tearing off flesh and nipples, bins of water for prisoners to be lowered into manacled and upside down, racks, electric chairs, cement strait-jackets with holes for instruments to be inserted.

Pinned to the wall was a list of rules. These included: "While getting lashes or electrification do not cry out. Sit still and await my orders. If you disobey any point of regulation you shall get 10 lashes or 5 shocks of electric discharge."

REGULATIONS

1. ANSWER AT ONCE
2. DON'T HIDE FACTS
3. WHEN GETTING LASHES OR ELECTRIC SHOCK DO NOT CRY OUT
4. SIT STILL, AWAIT ORDERS
5. DON'T PRETEND TO BE INNOCENT
6. DON'T MAKE EXCUSES
7. IF YOU DISOBEY YOU GET 10 LASHES OR 5 ELECTRIC SHOCKS

chamber of horrors

Each day the boy lay chained in terror in his cell, expecting every minute to be taken away for torture. Speaking was not allowed but there were cracks in the brick partitions and pressing close to these it was possible to whisper without the guards hearing. In the next cell the boy heard a voice praying — but he was not praying in the ancient language of the monks.

He seemed to be talking to God, just as the boy spoke to the Black Swan. "Who are you speaking to?" the boy whispered.

"I am praying to our Saviour — a simple prayer that He taught us."

"Who is this saviour?" the boy asked "Will He help us?"

Through the thin wall came the reply. "Long ago the compassion of God was revealed through a child born in the City. He called God his Father and some people call Him the Son of God. But that is just a way of explaining how God dwelled in Him — as He does in each of us."

whispers

"Oh, I've heard all about that!" protested the boy with disappointment as he remembered the executioner's story. "He was murdered. Why do you still pray to Him? How can He help now?"

"By His example," the priest continued, "Growing up in the City among ordinary people He understood our problems, our needs, our fears. He urged everyone to live a simple life, showing care and consideration, and to rediscover harmony with God. He suffered and He shares our suffering."

"That's what the great Guru preached," the boy exclaimed, remembering the old monk's teaching. "He called it the Middle Way." "The great Guru" explained the priest, "revealed the path to ENLIGHTENMENT, but for many of us this is hard to achieve no matter how many times we are re-born. It's like the game of Ropes and Ladders," he suggested. "The rope is the long gradual path to Enlightenment needing many re-births. The ladder offered by our Saviour is a short cut, revealing God's mercy for us."

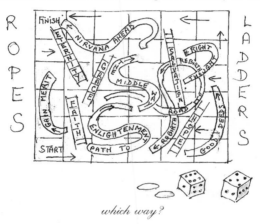

which way?

"But they killed your Saviour — just as they'll kill us," whispered the boy, stifling his tears. "How can He save us when He's dead?" "It was a sacrifice," replied the priest softly, sensing the boy's terror. "He sacrificed His life in exchange for God's mercy to mankind." "How?" sobbed the boy, "How can one life equal all mankind." "We believe it was God in Him that was the sacrifice. God dying for man. And He overcame death." "As a ghost?" asked the boy, astonished. "No, but to show us we have to die to be reborn. His promise was for us to be reunited with God forever — as God always intended."

"I believe in a Garden," the boy answered slowly, "where I came from and where it was promised I will return to."

After a pause he heard the priest reply, "Before our Saviour died He promised to send us a Comforter, a Guide, to remain with us. We call this friend the Holy Spirit who will always help us somehow when we are in need."

sacrifice

"Do you know about the Garden?" the boy whispered. He waited a moment, almost scared to continue, and then he poured out his story — about the Garden and the Black Swan and how he came to the City.

"I think your Black Swan is a messenger of God," said the priest, "the breath and inspiration of the Godhead. Trust him."

At that moment the guards returned, unlocked the priest's door and started to kick him and shout crude insults at him. "Tomorrow you will wish you had never been born," they called back as they left, slamming the cell door behind them.

The boy didn't care who heard him. He had to know. "How did they kill Him?" He shouted through the wall.

take that

"They whipped Him and tortured Him," cried back the priest. "They made Him haul a heavy post outside the city and nailed Him to it and hung Him up for everyone to see Him die, mocking and tormenting Him. And He called out for them to be forgiven!"

"Where did He die?" asked the boy. "Have I been there?"

"It doesn't matter where He died, because our Saviour lived and died for *all* people in *all* places in *all* time; past, present and to come. So that the sacrifice and the salvation are equally available to everyone everywhere."

As the boy grappled with these strange concepts, he sensed comprehension slowly growing within him. "Forgiveness is for everyone? No matter how terrible their crimes? How can that be?"

forgive?

"It must be," emphasised the priest, "for the heart of God reaches into the heart of everyone, tortured and torturer alike."

"But if God loved the world why does He let such terrible things happen?"

"God is a sacred mystery — but His compassion was revealed in our Saviour, who declared He came to the world not to judge us, but to save us. When He saw children enslaved and people suffering He was very angry. He said 'offences will always be done, but cursed be those who commit them.' "

"But you said everyone will be forgiven?"

"May be forgiven," corrected the priest. "The spirit of forgiveness is shared alike by the giver and the reciever. It is essential for all who set out on the road to Enlightenment, for all who wish to discover their immortal soul. The power of God is compassion," continued the priest. "It is a strength that doesn't interfere but is always there when we most need it. God did not even spare Himself — living and dying to show us the path to follow."

Then the guards returned and dragged the priest away. The boy listened to the sound of his body bumping down the stairs.

towed away

Knowing he would be tortured the next day the boy wept in terror. But even his sobs had to be silent otherwise the guards would lash him. As the boy lay chained to the floor groaning in terror, unable even to control his bowels for fear — he suddenly felt a breath of air and something soft as a feather brush his face.

Instead of a stench of mess and urine this was a breeze from the heart of the forest filled with fragrance. Out of the soft dark he heard the familiar voice of the Black Swan whispering, "Do not look forward to what might happen tomorrow. The same everlasting Father will take care of you. Either He will shield you from suffering or He will give you unfailing strength to bear it."

The boy felt the Swan's wing shielding him. "Do not be afraid for you are mine. Wherever you are, I am at your side. You are mine, my child, and I love you with a precious love."

hold me

The next morning as the boy was led to the interrogation room he saw the priest through an open door. The man, chained to a bed frame, was hardly recognisable. His face was battered and bloody, his lips torn and swollen. Lying on his side he recognised the boy. "Try to forgive them," he gasped. "It will put you beyond their reach to hurt you. What they do to the body does not matter. It is the soul that will fly."

Then the door slammed shut and he could only hear the terrible mechanical sounds of torture, interspersed with grunts and screams, going on within.

The guards wrapped a heavy chain around the boy's neck and pushed him into a room to be photographed.

smile please

The walls were lined with photographs, each one with a number and a date. The boy's polaroid print was stuck up on the wall. As he looked the boy recognised many of the faces staring back at him; the explorer, the banker, the builder, the woodseller, the monk from the temple, the trader from the yard, the painter, the blind musician, the foreign lady. All had been photographed and numbered before being tortured.

Outside in the yard a truck horn sounded. The truck was already being loaded up with its human cargo. There was no time for the boy to be interrogated. Just before the prison gates opened the broken body of the priest was dragged out and dumped on board. One eye had been torn out but his remaining eye stared at the boy. He tried to speak. "Death will not defeat us," he whispered, before one of the guards smashed a spade over his head.

day trip to ... ?

Among the people crowded into the truck the boy recognised familiar faces. The foreign lady, despite a black eye, looked as defiant as ever. The elderly monk, his safron robe torn and his face bruised, managed a kindly smile. "We are on the way to Enlightenment," he said softly. "Try not to be afraid. Your suffering is my suffering. Your joy will be my joy."

Hunched up together in the truck, too weak or wounded to respond, the boy saw so many of the people he had met in the City. There, staring out, stood the painter who had claimed to be a stealer of light, and looking strangely bemused the banker who had lost faith in money. The explorer, the blind musician, they were all there together. "We are going on a picnic, my dear," the foreign lady declared, firmly clasping the boy's hand. "A picnic in the country."

The Killing Fields

The truck drove down a street newly named after a hero of the revolution. It crossed a bridge and turned off along a dirt track into the rice fields. Soon it stopped and everyone was ordered or pulled out. The field was full of pits. There were pieces of torn clothing and crushed bones everywhere. A pack of wild dogs watched from the bushes. The prisoners were handed spades and ordered to dig a pit.

When this was deep enough they were lined up one by one, smashed over the head with the spade and thrown into the pit. There were some babies. These were torn from their mothers and thrown into the air to be speared with bayonets, or held by their feet and smashed against a tree to break their heads. Everyone was looking at the ground, weeping or praying.

dig!

With a great effort the boy forced his head back and stared up at the sky. Dark lowering clouds blacked out the flat horizon, but as he looked, trying to ignore the sickly thuds of the bludgeoning spades, he saw a gleam of golden light edge the clouds and cast an unexpected glow of brightness over the landscape — over the flat green rice fields and the muddy river beyond.

And in that instant the landscape transformed; the river narrowed, hills and forests rose up from the plain. He saw fruit bats hanging from the topmost branches, cooling themselves in the breeze, and he saw elephants rolling in the shallows. And looking further off he saw the great cataract cascading into the green forest. Above the cataract he noticed a dark dot in the sky growing steadily larger.

but ...

Then a voice that seemed to be part of the glow of light spoke to him.

"Do not be afraid. I have called you by name. You are mine."

Now he knew that the light and the sky and everything around him, even himself, were all a part of the word of God.

His bruised and haggard features broke into a smile once again as the boy watched the Black Swan beating its great wings through the blue vigour of the sky, coming to take him home.

going home ..

... the end ...

*The author, who has lived in Thailand a number of years,
does volunteer work in Cambodia and Indonesia.*

*One of the hopes of this little book is to raise money for
charities involved in helping children who, through no fault
of their own, are victims of poverty, war, persecution and sickness.*

All royalties will go to
The Center for the Protection of Children's Rights Foundation,
an affiliate of the Foundation for Children
185/16 Charansanitwong 12 Rd, Tha Phra District,
Bangkok Yai, Bangkok 10600, Thailand
Tel: (662) 412-1196, 412-0739, 864-1421 Fax: (662) 412-9833
Email: cpcr@internetksc.th.com

*Readers are also invited to make a small contribution. Those
living overseas will have similar charities they can help, including*
The Tibet Relief Fund, 114/115 Tottenham Court Road,
London WIP 9HL, U.K.,
*which helps the support and education
of Tibetan refugee children.*